To Michael, Cameron, Paisley, and Julia, thank you for being the reason I always keep dreaming. You inspire me every day. I love you to the moon and back and more than that, three times around and triple that!

To Allison, thank you for providing such amazing illustrations that bring this story to life.

www.mascotbooks.com

Chickens! Chickens! Everywhere!

©2022 Samantha Loza. All Rights Reserved. No part of this publication may be reproduced, stored in a retrieval system or transmitted in any form by any means electronic, mechanical, or photocopying, recording or otherwise without the permission of the author.

For more information, please contact:
Mascot Books
620 Herndon Parkway, Suite 320
Herndon, VA 20170
info@mascotbooks.com

Library of Congress Control Number: 2021919051

CPSIA Code: PRT1221A
ISBN-13: 978-1-63755-250-6

Printed in the United States

CHICKENS! CHICKENS! EVERYWHERE!

Samantha Loza

Illustrated by Allison Giles

Mom woke me up today with a surprise. "Okay Cameron, close your eyes."

I held them tightly closed. "Is it a toy? A bike? Some clothes?"

And then, **CHICKENS,** six of them!

CHICKENS! CHICKENS! EVERYWHERE! I couldn't help but want to stare.
Dad built a house for them to share. It's called a coop and they live in there.

He made it out of wood and wire, and they can lay
in a nest when they get tired.

We have to keep it pretty clean, and so that we don't step in poop, we wear our cool rain boots.

CHICKENS! CHICKENS! EVERYWHERE!

They're in my room,

they climb my stairs.

They roam outside most of the day.
Mommy says they are free range.
That means they are free to roam about,
but only if we let them out.

CHICKENS! CHICKENS! EVERYWHERE!

Did you know chickens have feathers instead of hair?

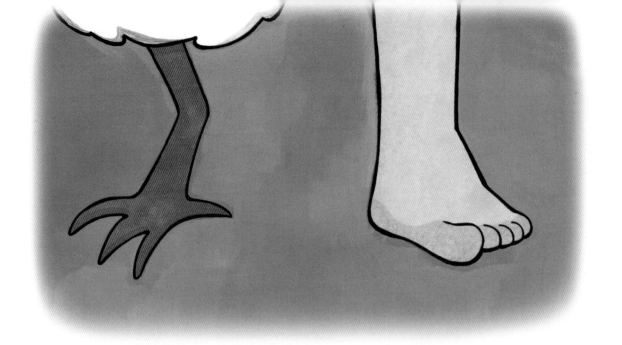

They also have claws, instead of feet.

And on their mouth, not lips, but a beak.

They tend to roam around in pairs.

I have a favorite;
I really adore her.
Mom says she's
the leader of the
pecking order.

I guess chickens have jobs like we do, and that means some boss others around when they need to.

In my house, sitting in my chair, one little hen likes to stay in there.

I caught her hiding from the others. She is timid and very shy; she won't come near me no matter how hard I try!

They get these bugs called mites
and lice. They peck at them
(that's the way they bite).

We wash them with a special spray. It
has vinegar, lavender, and lemongrass,
and it's even better than a bath!

They play with me and walk over my tummy.

Plus, they give us eggs, so fresh and yummy.

They are the coolest pets I've
ever seen, and if you're a chicken,
my backyard is the place to be!

ABOUT THE AUTHOR

Samantha Loza is from the Bay Area and enjoys reading and writing stories for children that are informative and fun. She has worked as an elementary school librarian and is currently on the path to become a teacher, so children's literature has a special place in her heart. When she is not writing, she enjoys reading to her three children. They love to come up with stories and hope to continue sharing them with readers in the future.